Clothes
La Ropa

by Mary Berendes • illustrated by Kathleen Petelinsek

Published in the United States of America by The Child's World®
1980 Lookout Drive • Mankato, MN 56003-1705
800-599-READ • www.childsworld.com

Acknowledgments
The Child's World®: Mary Berendes, Publishing Director
The Design Lab: Kathleen Petelinsek, Design and Page Production

Language Adviser: Ariel Strichartz

Library of Congress Cataloging-in-Publication Data
Berendes, Mary.
 Clothes = La ropa / by Mary Berendes ; illustrated by Kathleen Petelinsek.
    p. cm. — (WordBooks = Libros de palabras)
 ISBN 978-1-59296-989-0 (library bound : alk. paper)
 1. Clothing and dress—Terminology—Juvenile literature. 2. Picture
dictionaries, English—Juvenile literature. 3. Picture dictionaries, Spanish—
Juvenile literature. I. Petelinsek, Kathleen. II. Title. III. Title: Ropa. IV. Series.
 GT518.B37 2008
 391—dc22   2007046564

tassel
la borla

cap
el gorro

earmuffs
las orejeras

mitten
el mitón

coat
el chaquetón

scarf
la bufanda

ski pants
los pantalones
de esquiar

zipper
la cremallera

boots
las botas

3

sleeve
la manga

sweater
el suéter

4

glove
el guante

headband
la diadema

collar
el cuello

blouse
la blusa

vest
el chaleco

buttons
los botones

5

umbrella
el paraguas

raincoat
el impermeable

boots
las botas

hat
el sombrero

pants
los pantalones

jeans
los jeans

shoelace
el cordón

8

buckle
la hebilla

pocket
el bolsillo

tennis shoes
los zapatos
de tenis

overalls
el mono

patch
el parche

9

sunglasses
las gafas de sol

flip-flops
las chancletas

towel
la toalla

sunscreen
el bronceador
con filtro solar

11

pattern
el diseño

stripes
las rayas

socks
los calcetines

blouse
la blusa

12

skirt
la falda

shoes
los zapatos

13

polka dots
los lunares

dresses
los vestidos

14

sun hat
el sombrero
para el sol

bows
los lazos

jumper
el jumper

sundress
la solera

tights
las medias

15

tank top
la camiseta
sin mangas

T-shirt
la camiseta

skort
el faldapantalón

shorts
los shorts

stitching
las puntadas

blanket
la manta

sandals
las sandalias

17

hat
el sombrero

suit
el traje

briefcase
el maletín

suspenders
los tirantes

tie
la
corbata

stripes
las rayas

belt
el cinturón

watch
el reloj

cuff
el puño

19

robe
la bata

nightgown
el camisón

slippers
las zapatillas

pajamas
los pijamas

21

earrings
los pendientes

necklace
el collar

ring
el anillo

bracelet
la pulsera

watch
el reloj

pendant
el colgante

gloves
los guantes

accessories
los accesorios

scarf
la bufanda

purse
el bolso

wallet
la cartera

tie
la corbata

key chain
el llavero

23

word list
lista de palabras

accessories	los accesorios	**purse**	el bolso
belt	el cinturón	**raincoat**	el impermeable
blanket	la manta	**ring**	el anillo
blouse	la blusa	**robe**	la bata
boots	las botas	**sandals**	las sandalias
bows	los lazos	**scarf**	la bufanda
bracelet	la pulsera	**shoelace**	el cordón
briefcase	el maletín	**shoes**	los zapatos
buckle	la hebilla	**shorts**	los shorts
buttons	los botones	**ski pants**	los pantalones de esquiar
cap	el gorro	**skirt**	la falda
clothes	la ropa	**skort**	el faldapantalón
coat	el chaquetón	**sleeve**	la manga
collar	el cuello	**slippers**	las zapatillas
cuff	el puño	**socks**	los calcetines
dress	el vestido	**stitching**	las puntadas
earmuffs	las orejeras	**stripes**	las rayas
earrings	los pendientes	**suit**	el traje
flip-flops	las chancletas	**sun hat**	el sombrero para el sol
flippers	las aletas	**sundress**	la solera
glove	el guante	**sunglasses**	las gafas de sol
hat	el sombrero	**sunscreen**	el bronceador con filtro solar
headband	la diadema	**suspenders**	los tirantes
jeans	los jeans	**sweater**	el suéter
jumper	el jumper	**swimsuit**	el traje de baño
key chain	el llavero	**tank top**	la camiseta sin mangas
mask	las gafas	**tassel**	la borla
mitten	el mitón	**tennis shoes**	los zapatos de tenis
necklace	el collar	**tie**	la corbata
nightgown	el camisón	**tights**	las medias
overalls	el mono	**towel**	la toalla
pajamas	los pijamas	**T-shirt**	la camiseta
pants	los pantalones	**umbrella**	el paraguas
patch	el parche	**vest**	el chaleco
pattern	el diseño	**wallet**	la cartera
pendant	el colgante	**watch**	el reloj
pocket	el bolsillo	**zipper**	la cremallera
polka dots	los lunares		